D1633302

For
Theo and Freya
D.A.

First published in 2013 by Scholastic Children's Books
Euston House, 24 Eversholt Street
London NW1 1DB
a division of Scholastic Ltd
www.scholastic.co.uk
London ~ New York ~ Toronto ~ Sydney ~ Auckland
Mexico City ~ New Delhi ~ Hong Kong

PB ISBN 978 1407 13595 3

1 3 5 7 9 10 8 6 4 2

Papers used by Scholastic Children's Books are made from wood grown in sustainable forests.

Snow Ponies

By Dawn Apperley

SCHOLASTIC

Just below the clouds, at the bottom of a snowy mountain, lay an enchanted valley. It was the perfect place to find snow ponies, and this is exactly where Misty and Nutmeg lived.

Like all snow ponies, they were very adventurous and loved to explore the secrets of the enchanted valley.

"Look, Nutmeg! Rainbows!" laughed Misty. "Let's leap over them!"
Shaking their sparkly manes and swooshing their shimmery
tails, the friends jumped up, up, up and all the way over the
rainbows. They landed beside a silvery stream.

As they bent their heads to take a sip of the cool water, the friends
saw something shiny, right in the middle of the babbling stream.
"I think it's a star!" gasped Misty, looking really closely.

"But stars don't belong in streams,"
said Nutmeg. "What shall we do with it?"
"Let's take the star to Wise Owl," said Misty.
"He knows everything."

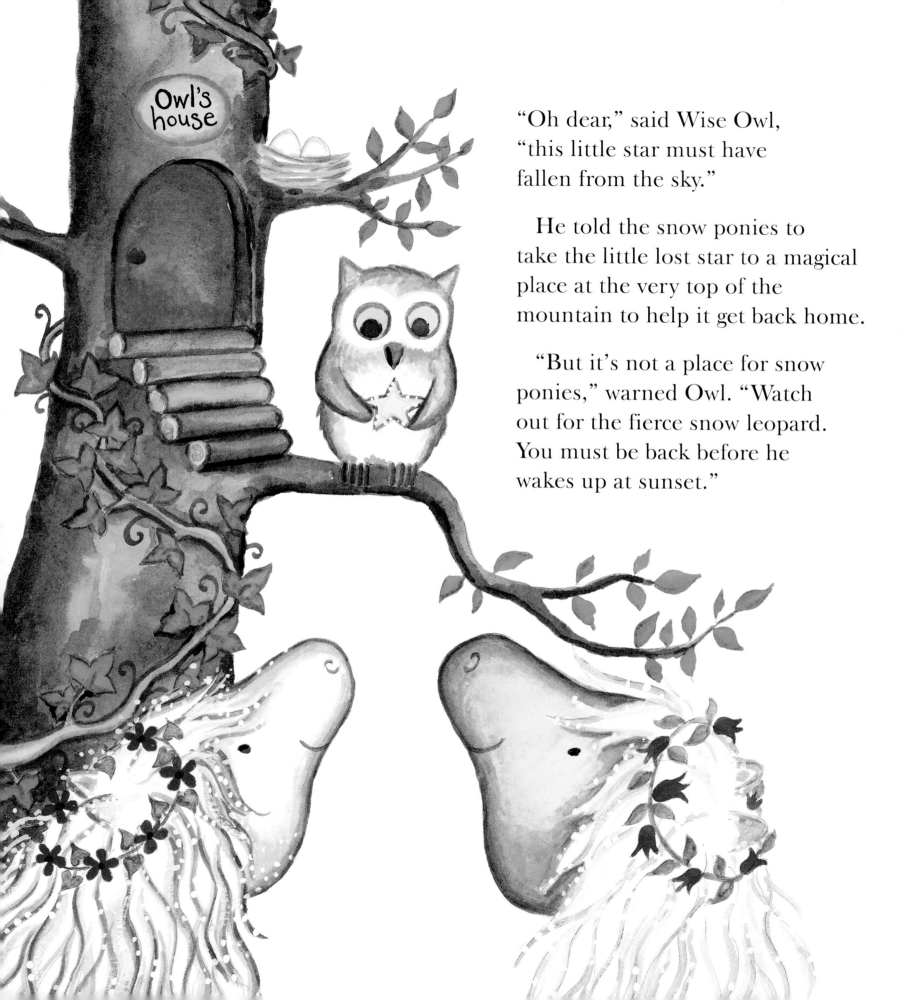

"Oh dear," said Wise Owl, "this little star must have fallen from the sky."

He told the snow ponies to take the little lost star to a magical place at the very top of the mountain to help it get back home.

"But it's not a place for snow ponies," warned Owl. "Watch out for the fierce snow leopard. You must be back before he wakes up at sunset."

"We're not scared!" said the brave snow ponies, and with two pony jumps they galloped off towards the tall mountain, carrying the little lost star.

"Don't worry, Little Star,"
said the snow ponies, "we'll take you home."
Higher and higher they climbed, towards the place
where snow ponies aren't supposed to go.
Soon they could see the pink, fluffy clouds.

As Misty and Nutmeg skipped and jumped through
the candyfloss clouds, they sang their favourite song:

We love to be snow ponies, and do snow pony things.
We shake our manes and shimmery tails and go snow-ponying.

At last, the clouds parted and, far above, the snow ponies could see the very top of the mountain. It was covered in crisp, white snow.

"You're almost home now, Little Star," said Nutmeg, as they kept on climbing through the soft, powdery snow.

"I wonder where the snow
leopard is?" asked Misty,
looking around nervously.
Very, very quietly,
very, very carefully,
and very, very slowly,
they climbed on, up towards
the magic place at the top
of the mountain.

"Look!" whispered Nutmeg.
"Leopard footprints!
He must be sleeping in this cave."
The brave snow ponies kept on going.
They had to save the little lost star!

At the top of the mountain, the snow ponies held the little star up as high as they could and waited...

In a flurry of stardust, a big star floated down and lovingly lifted the little star up in its arms.

"Goodbye, Little Star," called Misty and Nutmeg.

The friends began the journey back down the icy mountain.

"Hurry," said Misty, "The sun is setting and the snow leopard will wake up soon."

Very, very quietly, and very, very carefully, they tip-toed past his cave.

Suddenly, the snow ponies stopped. Thick clouds covered
the ground ahead and the path was nowhere to be seen.

"Which way should we go?" asked Misty.

"I think we're lost!" Nutmeg gasped.

"I want to go home," cried Misty.
"Let's sing the snow pony song," said Nutmeg,
rubbing Misty's nose. "That will
make us feel braver."

We love to be snow ponies, and do snow pony things,
we shake our manes and shimmery tails and go snow-ponying.

Then the snow ponies heard a low and scary growl. "It's the snow leopard!" whimpered Misty. "He's awake!"

"Quick! Let's hide," whispered Nutmeg.

The friends hid amongst the clouds as they watched the leopard creep closer and closer…

Just then, something sparkled above their heads. It was the little star! Then another star appeared … and another … and another…

Soon a ring of twinkling stars danced above the snow ponies' heads.

"They want us to follow them," smiled Nutmeg.

The sparkling stars led the snow ponies back through
the thick, fluffy clouds, down the steep mountain path
and away from the scary snow leopard. Soon they
were safely back home amongst the leafy
trees of the enchanted valley —
the perfect place for snow ponies.